HEIDI

Illustrated by RENE CLOKE

AWARD PUBLICATIONS – LONDON

One hot day, a little girl and a young woman, carrying a bundle, climbed up a steep mountain path in Switzerland. "Good morning, Dete," called a friend as they passed her cottage door, "Where are you taking little Heidi?" "I am taking her to live with her grandfather," answered Aunt Dete, "I have looked after her for five years, now it is his turn."

Heidi was feeling very hot; she was wearing two dresses and a red woollen shawl, for all her clothes would not go in the bundle.

While the women were talking, Heidi wandered off by herself.

A boy was climbing the mountain with a herd of goats and Heidi noticed how easily he walked with bare feet; she threw off her two dresses, her shawl and her shoes and stockings.

"That's better!" she cried and ran off to join the goatherd. They soon made friends, laughing and talking as they leaped over the rocks with the goats.

When Aunt Dete joined them, Peter,
the goatherd, carried Heidi's clothes
and they all went up to the hut on the
side of the mountain.

"Good evening, grandfather," said Heidi.

"What is the meaning of this?" asked the old man.

"You must look after her now," said Aunt Dete, "she is your
grandchild. Good-bye, Heidi," and she hurried away down the
mountain path.

Grandfather didn't look
very pleased but he told
Heidi to pick up her
bundles and come
inside the hut.

There was one big, tidy room with a
ladder in the corner; Heidi climbed up
and looked into a hay-loft.

"I should like to sleep up here" she
cried, "I can see down into the valley
from the window!"

Grandfather laughed and helped her
to make her bed in the hay.

When they had had supper together, milk, bread and cheese, grandfather showed Heidi his two goats which Peter had brought back from the mountain.

"Their names are Little Swan and Little Bear," he told her.

Every day, Heidi went up the mountain with Peter and the goats. They took bread and cheese with them and a little bowl for a drink of goat's milk.

Heidi was very happy skipping about picking the lovely flowers which grew amongst the rocks and staring in amazement at the great bird which circled above them.

"It's nest is high up in the mountain top,"
Peter told her, "higher than even the
goats can climb."
He had a busy time looking after Heidi as
well as the herd of goats and was
glad when it was time for dinner
and a rest on the grass.

Autumn came and then winter and one day Peter did not come for the goats; snow had fallen in the night and grandfather had to shovel it away from the door.

When Peter was able to reach the hut he was glad to come in and warm his feet by the fire.

"Well," said grandfather, "I suppose you go to school now that the snow is here and you cannot take the goats up the mountain?"

"Yes," answered Peter and he did not look very happy about it. Then he told them that his grandmother would like Heidi to go and see her.

"She is blind," said Peter, "and she and my mother are very lonely for not many people come up the mountain in the winter."

So one bright morning,
grandfather took Heidi
in his sleigh down the
mountainside and left her at Peter's hut.
It was very dark and shabby inside; the grandmother was
sitting by the fire with her spinning wheel and Peter's mother
was patching an old waistcoat.

They were both delighted when Heidi walked in.

"Grandfather brought me in his sleigh," she explained.

The grandmother wanted to know just what the little girl looked like, so Peter's mother described her while Heidi stood by the fire.

"The shutters on the window are broken," said the grandmother, "but there is no one to mend things, so the hut is falling to pieces."

"I will ask grandfather to help you," said Heidi.

Peter's mother was surprised when Heidi's grandfather came the next day and mended the broken shutters.

"Who would have believed it? He has never helped us before," she said.

"It must be Heidi's doing," declared the grandmother.

Heidi was very happy in the mountains, playing with Peter and the goats, helping her grandfather and visiting Peter's blind grandmother.

But one day plans were made for her to go and live in the big town as a companion for Clara, a little invalid girl.

Grandfather was very angry about the arrangement and Peter felt sad to lose his friend.

When Heidi arrived at the grand town house, Sebastian, the footman, took her to the room where Clara lay on her couch.

Clara's governess did not like Heidi's plain country clothes and thought the little girl was stupid because she had never learned any lessons.

"Can you read and write?" she asked.

"No," answered Heidi.

"I am afraid you are not the sort of companion we want for Clara," said the governess crossly; she looked at Heidi's untidy luggage and shook her head disapprovingly.

But Clara liked Heidi and said they would enjoy doing lessons together.

Heidi told her all about grandfather and Peter and his mother and grandmother and the goats.

When Heidi looked out of her window the next day, she saw a great tower in the distance with a gold ball on top.

"I must go and look for it," she said and out she ran.

But the streets were crowded with people and Heidi could not find her way to the tower; everyone seemed to be in a hurry and she did not like to ask the way.

Then, at the corner of the street, she saw a boy with a monkey and an organ on his back; he said he would help her and together they found the tower with the golden ball on top.

Heidi was taken to the top of the tower and saw the big city lying below.
The old man who lived in the tower showed her his cat and kittens.

"May I have a kitten?" asked Heidi.
"Take two now," said the old man, "and I will bring the others to your house to-morrow."

The boy with the monkey and the old man with the basket of kittens came to the house the next day and brought a turtle as well.

Clara gave the boy some money for helping Heidi and he played a tune for her on his organ.

But when the governess came into the room she was very cross indeed and wanted to send the animals away.

"Heidi must be punished," she declared.

"Wait until Papa comes home," pleaded Clara, "he will say what must be done."

The kind footman, Sebastian, said he would take care of the kittens and he made a comfortable bed for them in a basket. When Clara's father came home he was so pleased to see what good friends Clara and Heidi had become that he did not mind the basketful of kittens.

He told the governess that Heidi must stay with them. "My mother is coming on a visit and will look after Heidi," he said.

Heidi loved Clara and tried hard with her lessons but she found them very difficult until Clara's grandmother came to stay with them and taught her to read. She gave her a beautiful story book but the pictures of goats and mountains made Heidi sad with longing for her home with grandfather.

The months passed by and Heidi became more and more homesick for the country air.

"You must send her back to her grandfather," the doctor told Clara's father.

Heidi was delighted to go back to the mountains and, when at last the long journey was over, she walked into Peter's hut with a basket of presents.

Peter's mother admired her fine clothes but Heidi said, "I will change into my old dress or grandfather won't know me!"

Grandfather was sitting outside his hut, smoking his pipe when Heidi ran up the path.

"Heidi, you have come back to me!" and he held out his arms to greet her.

"Grandfather!" she cried, throwing down her basket and hugging him, "how glad I am to be home again!"

After supper, Heidi heard Peter bringing home the goats and ran out to greet them.

"It's good to see you again," laughed Peter as Heidi stroked Little Bear and Little Swan.

When winter came, grandfather and Heidi went down the mountain to live in the village; Heidi often visited Peter's mother and read to his grandmother.

"You will be able to go to school with Peter, now," said grandfather.

Peter was not fond of school and could not learn to read, so, one day, Heidi thought of a plan.

"I will teach you your letters so that you can read to your grandmother when the snow is too deep for me to reach the hut. Just think how pleased she will be!"

This made Peter try much harder and before long he could read quite well.

"Who would have thought it possible?" said his mother.

"Heidi taught me," answered Peter.

Grandmother looked happy for now there would always be someone to read to her.

Peter felt very pleased with himself and on the days when Heidi did not come to the hut he often read his books to his mother and grandmother.

Grandfather and Heidi went back to the mountain
hut when the spring came and one happy
day Clara and her grandmother came to see them.
Clara was carried in a sedan chair while grandmother rode a
horse; Clara's invalid chair was brought as well so that she
could be wheeled into the hut.

"I wish I could run about over the rocks as you do, Heidi,"
said Clara.

"Why not let Clara stay here with us?" suggested grandfather, "she would soon get well and strong."

So when grandmother went home that evening, she left Clara
with Heidi and her grandfather to enjoy the fine mountain air.

Clara and Heidi had a very happy time together but Peter was angry and jealous; he thought that Heidi would spend all her time with Clara now.

"They will sit talking together," he grumbled, "and Heidi won't come with me when I take the goats up the mountain." One morning, when no one was about, he pushed Clara's chair over the rocks and it rolled over the rocks out of sight. "Now, perhaps, she will go away," he thought.

"Why, my chair has gone!" cried Clara.

"Never mind," said grandfather and, taking a pile of rugs, he carried Clara up the mountain to picnic with the others.

The goat's milk and fine mountain air soon did Clara so much good that her cheeks grew as plump and rosy as Heidi's.
After a time she was able to walk; slowly at first but a little further every day as she became stronger and stronger.
Peter would not join the little girls' picnic; he was afraid that they might find out about the lost chair.
"How strange Peter has become," said Heidi, "I expect he has been up to some mischief."

When Clara's father and grandmother came to take her home it was a wonderful surprise to see the little girl running to meet them.

"I can hardly believe my eyes!" cried grandmother.

"I broke the chair," Peter confessed, "but Clara doesn't need it now; she can walk as well as we can!"

Clara was sorry to say good-bye and leave the mountain hut.

"You will come again," said Heidi, "and next time you will be able to walk and run about with us all the time. Good-bye! Good-bye!"